The Paper Chain

Claire Blake • Eliza Blanchard • Kathy Parkinson

Illustrated by Kathy Parkinson

This book is dedicated to Matt and Jay and to families
like theirs, our inspiration from the very start.

My family loves to do things outside — especially when the weather is warm. That's why we like summer best of all. But last summer things were different.

One warm spring day my little brother Marcus and I were digging a deep hole in our back yard. Dad came out and said, "Ben, Marcus, please come inside now." After a few more digs we went in.

Dear Readers:

After her cancer diagnosis, author Claire Blake tried to help her young sons understand her illness and noticed a lack of children's stories. Trained in early childhood education, she knew the healing power of stories, especially for children. Her desire to help families like her own was the motivating force behind this book.

A life-threatening illness in a family is an issue we need seriously and urgently to talk about with children. Often we don't attend to children when such a crisis occurs, or not in a timely fashion. This story offers a place to start such a discussion in a sensitive and thoughtful way; it provides a vehicle to open up a dialogue about a difficult but important topic.

It is important to remember that the treatments and outcome in this story may not be similar to those of other patients with breast or other cancers. Talking with the medical team will ensure that both the patient and his or her family will get the best possible advice about available treatments and choices. Sharing information and feelings about health issues with family and with supportive friends can be a healthy way to deal with the stress of a serious illness.

Dr. Eli Newberger
Director, Family Development Program
Children's Hospital, Boston

Mom said, "When I had my check-up this morning, the doctor said I need an operation. I'll have to stay in the hospital for a few nights, but Dad will be here and maybe Aunt Marie will come too."

Marcus said "Okay, Mom, but I'm going with you!" Dad told him healthy kids weren't allowed to sleep in the hospital. "It won't be for long, Marc. Don't worry." Mom, Marcus and I made a paper chain with two links for each day she'd be gone, one each for us to tear off at night.

Mom left one morning before Dad took us to school. Even before lunch I felt sad.

"I miss my mom. She went to the hospital," I told my teacher.

"I'm sure you miss her, but you can call her when you get home," she said. When I got home Dad dialed her number for us and we talked a long time. Then I felt better.

We decided to plant some pansies for Mom. The next day Aunt Marie was there when we got home from school. We all cleaned Mom's room and made a "Welcome Home!" sign.

"Mom's coming home soon!" I told Marcus when we were tearing links from our paper chain.

Finally, she came home! Boy, was I glad to see my same old Mom! Marcus said, "I want to see your booboo!" Later, when Dad helped change her bandage, she let us see her stitches. Lucky Mom... she wasn't allowed to take a bath for a week!

It hurt Mom when we hugged her because of the stitches. When Marcus cried, "I need to sit in your lap!" Dad invented a Yarn Hug. He took a fat piece of red yarn, wrapped it around Mom, then around us. It felt goofy but good, too.

Mom had to nap every day to feel stronger. One day she went back to the doctor. Mom told us what she had was called cancer. "Cancer is something growing inside the body that it doesn't need," she said.

"Can I catch it from you?" I asked.

"No, you can't catch cancer from other people," Mom told us, "and you can't give it to anyone. It's not like a cold."

A special doctor would give Mom strong medicines to help her get rid of the cancer. "Do you have to go to the hospital again?" I cried. "You hardly played outside all summer. When will you get better?"

"I don't know. Cancer is hard to cure, but we're doing all we can to help me. You and Marcus are an important part of my team."

Mom took us to meet her oncologist, Dr. Miller, who knew all about cancer. Dr. Miller was very friendly. She told us Mom would take a lot of medicines. This is called chemotherapy.

Dr. Miller told us Mom might be very tired again, or even sick, after her treatments. "Kind of like you feel when you have a bad case of the flu," she said.

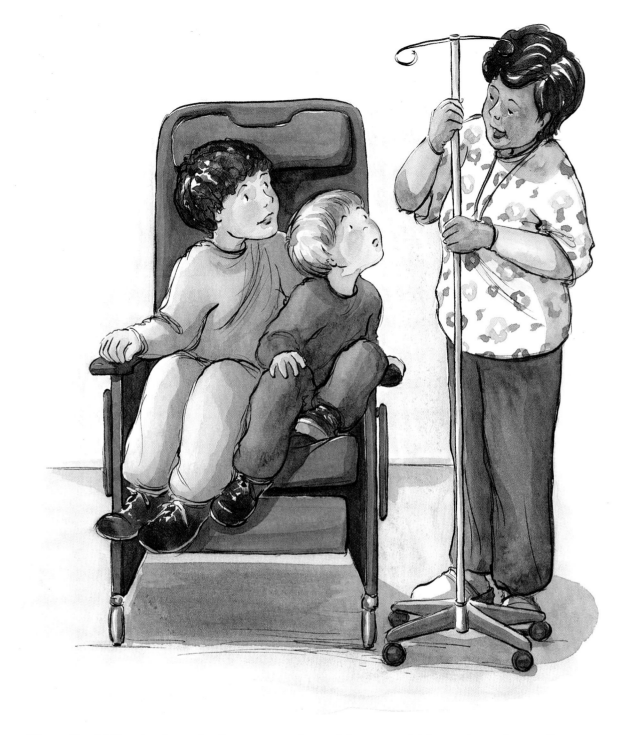

Then Dr. Miller took us to the room where Mom would have her chemotherapy. The nurse let us sit in the big chair that Mom would use and showed us the long shiny pole on wheels that holds a bag of medicine.

"It works like a shot in the arm," the nurse said, "but the medicine drips into your body slowly. It can take a few hours."

Marcus said, "I don't think I could sit still for Drip Medicine!"

That afternoon Marcus and I got out our bears. We called our game "Dr. Bear" and I made my bear a badge with "Chemicals Doctor" on it. Marcus' bear was the patient, Mom Bear. My bear listened while Mom Bear asked a zillion questions about her cancer.

Dr. Bear said, "These chemicals will help you get better. Take this!" and gave Mom Bear lots and lots of shots.

A while later the chemotherapy made Mom's hair start to fall out, and then she looked bald. At first she wore a scarf, but we didn't like it, so she got a wig. Her wig looked just like her regular hair did.

Mom needed a lot of rest, and this time she felt too sick to eat, so we brought her pillows and the mail. At first it was fun to help, but then it got boring. All she'd do with us was read and watch TV. Dad would play a little when he got home, but then he'd need to start dinner.

One afternoon we were playing a game and Marcus wouldn't play by the rules, so I pushed him. That started a fight. Mom shouted, "Stop that right now, you two!" When she stood up to yell, I felt very frightened. She sent us to our rooms and Marcus cried.

I stomped up the stairs. The first thing I did was rip up my drawing of Dr. Bear and Mom Bear. I could hear Marcus still crying next door. "Be quiet!" I yelled.

When we got quiet, Mom called us down. She said, "I'm sorry I'm so tired. It's okay to be angry, but we all have to use our words, so hit pillows, not people." Punching the sofa pillow, she shouted, "I'm sick and tired of being sick and tired!" We punched those pillows and laughed until we couldn't stand up.

After Halloween, Mom could eat like she used to. She'd make popcorn and cocoa after school. In December, Dad put lights on our tree and then Dad, Marcus and I put on all the ornaments. Mom watched from her favorite chair. "It's the most beautiful tree I've ever seen!" she told us. We had the coziest day that day.

In January, Dad asked Marcus and me to choose new chores. Marcus would set the table for breakfast and I'd set it for dinner. We both helped fix our lunches for school. Dad did the dishes and we helped put them away. Once I said I didn't feel like it, and he put soapsuds on my nose. "You know, every little bit helps Ben!"

When the chemotherapy was done, Mom told us she had to have radiation treatments. "Having radiation is like having an x-ray. Remember when you fell out of the treehouse last year, Ben, and your leg was x-rayed?"

"Yeah," I told Marcus, "it didn't hurt a bit." When we asked to see the machine they'd use, Mom said she'd take us.

Mom had to go for radiation every day, and it made her very tired. Every day Marcus asked, "Who'll pick me up from school today?" He was annoying, but I was glad he asked. When she answered, "Kris will," we'd cheer because he was our favorite babysitter.

We took long walks with Kris. We'd find things to bring home to Mom. On rainy days we invented interesting projects in the kitchen. With Kris, there was always something fun.

It was time to get our vegetable garden ready. Mom was too tired, but Dad said, "If you'll help me, we can turn the dirt and plant this weekend." When it was finished, I asked if she could at least take a walk with us.

"I'm so sorry, not today. I'm just too tired."

I stomped around for a while. Then I got out my bike and rode around the driveway, and I felt better.

When Marcus came out we chalked a huge maze on the blacktop.

When we came inside Mom said, "I'm proud of you boys. I know you're disappointed. I am too, when we can't do some things we love to do. But we can do others."

We cuddled together and Mom made up a story about the bears.

Mom's hair was slowly growing back.

"It looks just like the baby chick's fur at school," said Marcus. I laughed.

"They have feathers, not fur, you silly!" I said. We rubbed Mom's fuzzy new hair for luck.

Mom didn't have to have radiation anymore! And she had energy for a walk. "Let's go for a hike!" she announced, so the whole family walked up the hill behind our house to the woods. Marcus and I played airplanes and zoomed around and around Mom and Dad.

On the way home, we found a young blue jay hopping around. It had fallen from its nest and couldn't fly back. Dad said, "You two can take it home and take care of it until it can fly. Do you want to try?"

At home, Dad and I made a nest out of his old T-shirt and a shoe box. Mom found an eye-dropper and we took turns feeding the bird.

28

Marcus put both our bears beside the nest and made a paper chain for the bird. "Don't worry," he told it, "in this many days you can go home from the hospital."

We had an ice cream celebration that night. It was the best ice cream party ever!

Mom gave us the yarn from our Yarn Hug. "To make the nest warm and cozy," she said. "I'll have to visit Dr. Miller to be sure the cancer hasn't come back, but I don't think we need this now," and she hugged me tight.